बिल्ली
Billi
cat

हाँ
Han
yes

नहीं
Nahi
no

रानी
Rani
queen

आलू गोबी
Aloo Gobi
spiced potato
and cauliflower

LAXMI'S MOOCH

For Laddoo & Pinni & all the little
kids out there with mooches.
—S.A.

To Sundus and Samya, for believing in me and my art.
—N.H.A.

Kokila
An imprint of Penguin Random House LLC, New York

First published in the United States of America by Kokila, an imprint of Penguin Random House LLC, 2021

Text copyright © 2021 by Shelly Anand
Illustrations copyright © 2021 by Nabi H. Ali

Kokila & colophon are registered trademarks of Penguin Random House LLC.

Visit us online at penguinrandomhouse.com.

Library of Congress Cataloging-in-Publication Data is available.

Manufactured in China
ISBN 9781984815651

1 3 5 7 9 10 8 6 4 2

Design by Jasmin Rubero
Text set in ITC Officina serif Std Book

The art for this book was created digitally.

LAXMI'S MOOCH

by Shelly Anand

illustrated by

Nabi H. Ali

Kokila

Hi! I'm Laxmi.

Come here. *Closer*.
You see that?
That's my mooch.

What's a mooch? you ask.
These little hairs
above my lip.

It's okay, you can look.

I never really thought about my mooch until the other day,
when my friends and I were playing farm animals at recess.

Zoe was a horse.

Noah was a cow.

And Zoe said, "Laxmi, you're a cat, OK?"
"I want to be a chicken!" I said.
"But you're the perfect cat! You have
these little hairs on your lip, like cat
whiskers," said Zoe.

"I do?" I asked.

"Meow!" said Noah. "Yeah, you have a little mustache like my dad."

My cheeks grew as hot as a steaming bowl of Mummy's aloo gobi.

I went to the bathroom after recess and looked in the mirror.

Zoe was right. I did look like a cat with small black whiskers.

I sat at my desk with my hand over my mouth so no one could see my mooch.

Everywhere I walked, I thought I heard kids whisper "meow."

The whole day, I kept noticing hair all over my body.

On my arms.

And legs.

And knuckles.

Even in the space
between my eyebrows!

When I got home that afternoon, Mummy asked, "How was school, beta?"

"Well, Zoe said I'd make a good cat," I said.

"Aww, you're my little billi," she said.

"No, Mummy! She was calling me hairy!"

"Huh, I thought we named you Laxmi," said Papa, looking up from the roti he was making on the stove.

"No, look. I'm hairy. I have hair all over my body. I have a mustache."

"Haan, I also have a mooch," said Mummy.

"But, Mummy, I thought mooches were just for boys, like Papa."

"Nahi! You know, we come from a long line of women with moochay," said Mummy.

"We do? Like who?"

"From Mughal empresses and stately ranis to village girls and city girls. Even your nani and cousin Radha.

"Everyone has a mooch, really."
"But I also have hair on my arms and legs. I have hair all over!"
Mummy shrugged. "Toh kya?"
"So what?! Hair is just for your head."

Mummy smiled. "Nahi, beta, we have hair everywhere."

"But why?"

"It protects you and keeps you warm. Just feel it—so nice and soft," she said.

"But look at this hair—between my eyebrows?"

"Yes, it's lovely, just like Frida Kahlo!" said Papa.

"Who?" I asked.

"Frida Kahlo—she was a famous artist from Mexico."

"Oh. I think it kind of looks like a caterpillar," I said.

"Caterpillars are the coolest, beta—they build cocoons and become butterflies!" said Papa.

"First I'm a billi and now I'm a butterfly?" I asked.

That night, I dreamed about Royal Bengal tigers prowling through the Sundarbans. Their long black whiskers danced in the hot breeze, and butterflies flew behind them, fluttering around their long tails.

The next day at recess, Zoe wanted to play farm animals again.
"Let's play jungle animals instead. I'm a tiger with my long
silky mooch!" I said.

"A long silky what?" said Zoe
"Mooch—it's Hindi for mustache."
"Well, what should I be?" asked Zoe.

I walked up to Zoe and got really close. I saw tiny blond hairs on her lip. Sure enough, she had a mooch too. "You should be a lion, with your shiny blond whiskers!" I whispered.

"I don't have whiskers!" Zoe said.

"Do too!" I said.

We both ran to the bathroom and looked in the mirror.
"I don't see anything," Zoe said.

"Move in closer," I told her.

She leaned in so close that her nose left a little smudge on the glass. "Oh," she said, and then slowly she smiled.

When we came out of the bathroom, Noah was waiting for us.

"Hey, what about me? Do I have a mooch?" he asked.

Zoe and I both looked, but we didn't see a single hair above his lip.

"Nope," said Zoe.

"Yeah, I don't see anything, Noah, but maybe we can draw one on for you? Until your real one comes in," I said.

"OK!" agreed Noah.

A small group of the other kids in our class crowded around as I carefully drew a mooch on Noah's lip.

"Me next!" said Savi.

Aa Bb Cc Dd Ee Ff
Gg Hh Ii Jj Kk Ll
Mm Nn Oo Pp Qq Rr
Ss Tt Uu Vv Ww Xx

"Me too, please! After Savi?" asked Timmy.

They lined up behind Noah for my world-class mooches.

"I don't need one. I already have some hair there." Lucha smiled proudly.

"So do I!" cheered Arazoo.

Pretty soon, everyone was showing off their mooches, real and drawn.

So will you show me yours?

मूँछ
Mooch
مونچھ

mustache

बेटा
Beta
بیٹا

child

तितली
Titli
تِتلی

butterfly

नानी
Nani
نانی

grandma

तो क्या
Toh Kya?
تو کیا

so what?

रोटी
Roti
روٹی

flatbread